First published in Scotland in 2018 by Mags2Publishing, 13 Annfield Terrace, Prestwick KA9 IPS

Text © Greta Yorke 2018

Illustrations © Maggie Bolton 2018

The right of Greta Yorke and Maggie Bolton to be identified as the author and illustrator of this work has been

asserted to them in accordance with the Copyright, Designs and Patents Act, 1988.

A CIP record of this title is available from the British Library.

ISBN 978-0-9932124-6-8

Printed and bound in Scotland

Design:

Studio H, Courtyard Studios, 128 Harbour Street, Irvine KA12 8PZ

tallwork@icloud.com

How the Pirates Turned the Tide

By Greta Yorke

Illustrated by Maggie Bolton

M ost grans come by bus or car, but not my gran, oh no! She zoomed up on her silver scooter. She had come to take me to the beach for a picnic. I put on my helmet and off we went.

It was great whizzing along behind Gran. We drove out of town, through the lumpy bumpy countryside and on to the splishy splashy sea.

Most grans would be happy to sit and watch me play, or read a book after we ate our picnic, but not my gran, oh no!

3

She spied some rowing boats. 'I haven't been on one of those since I was your age,' she said. 'Come on, lets go!

BOATS FOR HIRE

4

Gran sat in the middle and rowed, while I leaned over trailing my hand in the icy water. 'Lets have a rest now,' said Gran and we lay back in the sunshine and fell asleep as the little boat gently rocked.

A loud roar wakened us. 'Heave to!' A creaky freaky pirate ship was high above us. Most grans would row away as fast as they could but not my gran, oh no!

'Wow, I've never been on a pirate ship. Come on,' she shouted, as she tied the rowing boat to the ship's rope ladder, grabbed my hand and hauled me up on board.

6

There was litter all over the deck and ragged pirates huddled behind the biggest, scariest man I'd ever seen, Captain Black. 'You're my prisoners now,' he roared.

Most grans would be frightened, but not my gran oh, no! She marched right up to him. 'Look at the state of your ship and your crew. You're a disgrace!' she said. The captain's face reddened and he scowled down on us.

'Get all this rubbish cleared up then get buckets, brushes and mops and swab that deck,' Gran ordered the pirates as she handed them black bin bags from her rucksack.

'But we're hungry, there's nothing to eat,' one protested. 'You clean, I'll see what's for eating, she replied and went off to the galley. 'Is she always like this?' Captain Black asked and I nodded.

PIZZA

8

She returned with potatoes, a few carrots and onions and announced 'there's plenty here'.

'Yuk, we hate that stuff,' said the captain, 'we like burgers and pizzas and chicken nuggets and chips.' 'We'll see about that! Your men are tired and lazy because they don't eat healthy food!' replied Gran. Captain Black muttered to himself as he steered the ship and I helped the pirates to tidy up and clean the ship.

9

Gran peeled and cut the vegetables then put them into a huge pot with water and stock cubes and some curry powder. 'That can simmer away nicely,' she said as she put the lid on the pot and went through to the bunks.

10

'These sheets need washing next,' she said as she pulled them off the beds. 'Get soapy water in those tubs,' she told two of the pirates, 'then get this bedding washed and hung up to dry.'

Gran got out her mobile phone and phoned home. She told mum I was having a sleep over with her and wouldn't be home for two or three nights.

We worked hard all day and at night time the ship was tidy and there was a pile of full bin bags. We dropped anchor and went for dinner.

11

12

Gran made the most delicious vegetable curry and rice. Everyone tucked in and enjoyed it. 'Can we have seconds?' asked one of the pirates and the others held up their plates.

'Tomorrow you can fish and I'll show you how to make a fish pie,' said Gran.

13

Gran and I settled into our bunks and she told me a bedtime story.

One by one the pirates came over to listen and one by one we went to sleep.

14

N ext day we anchored near an island and Gran,
Captain Black and I went to the market for
fresh fruit and vegetables.

15

'Who needs takeaways?' Gran said when we returned. A bucket of fish sat by the galley door and a bucket of seaweed sat beside it.

'Well done you lot,' smiled Gran, 'now tidy up and get your washing done before playtime.' 'Playtime?' chorused the pirates. 'Just wait and see,' winked Gran.

16

After work was finished she helped them set up circuit stations with jumping, skipping and hoola-hooping round the deck.

'You've got lots of energy now because you ate well and slept well,' she told them as they darted round.

RUNNING

beans

carrots

17

I played with the pirates while Gran showed the others how to make fish pie and fruit salad.

HULA HOOP

JUMPING

SKIPPING

18

'That food was yummy,' beamed Captain Black later as he cleared his plate, 'you really are a good cook.' Gran winked at me.

The pirates then told us how Deadeye Dan always managed to find them and steal their food and treasure.

'His men are nasty and much stronger than us,' one complained.

'But you'll soon be stronger if you eat good food, exercise and get plenty of sleep,' Gran said.

20

Gran kept the fish heads and tails and vegetable skins which made stink bombs to fire at Deadeye Dan. 'Will you tell us a story again tonight?' they asked. 'After you've tidied up and cleaned your teeth,' said Gran.

Captain Black anchored the ship and came to hear the story too and one by one, they fell asleep.

21

smelly rubbish

The pirates and I fished, tidied, caught lots of ghost gear then set up an obstacle race while Gran wrote her recipes at the front of a notebook and her bedtime stories at the back. We had spicy fishcakes and apple crumble for dinner.

22

N ext day Gran gave the "Feed and Read" notebook to Captain Black. We said goodbye to the pirates, climbed back down into the rowing boat and Gran rowed back to shore.

23

Most grans are happy to relax and take things easy, but I'm glad not my gran oh no!

24

What happens next...

The Pirates are
successful gardeners.

The Pirates filter
their own water.

The Pirates clean up the seas
and recycle the waste.